❯THE STORY OF A PIONEER GIRL❮

Rachel's Journal

D0565089

3¢ US POSTAGE

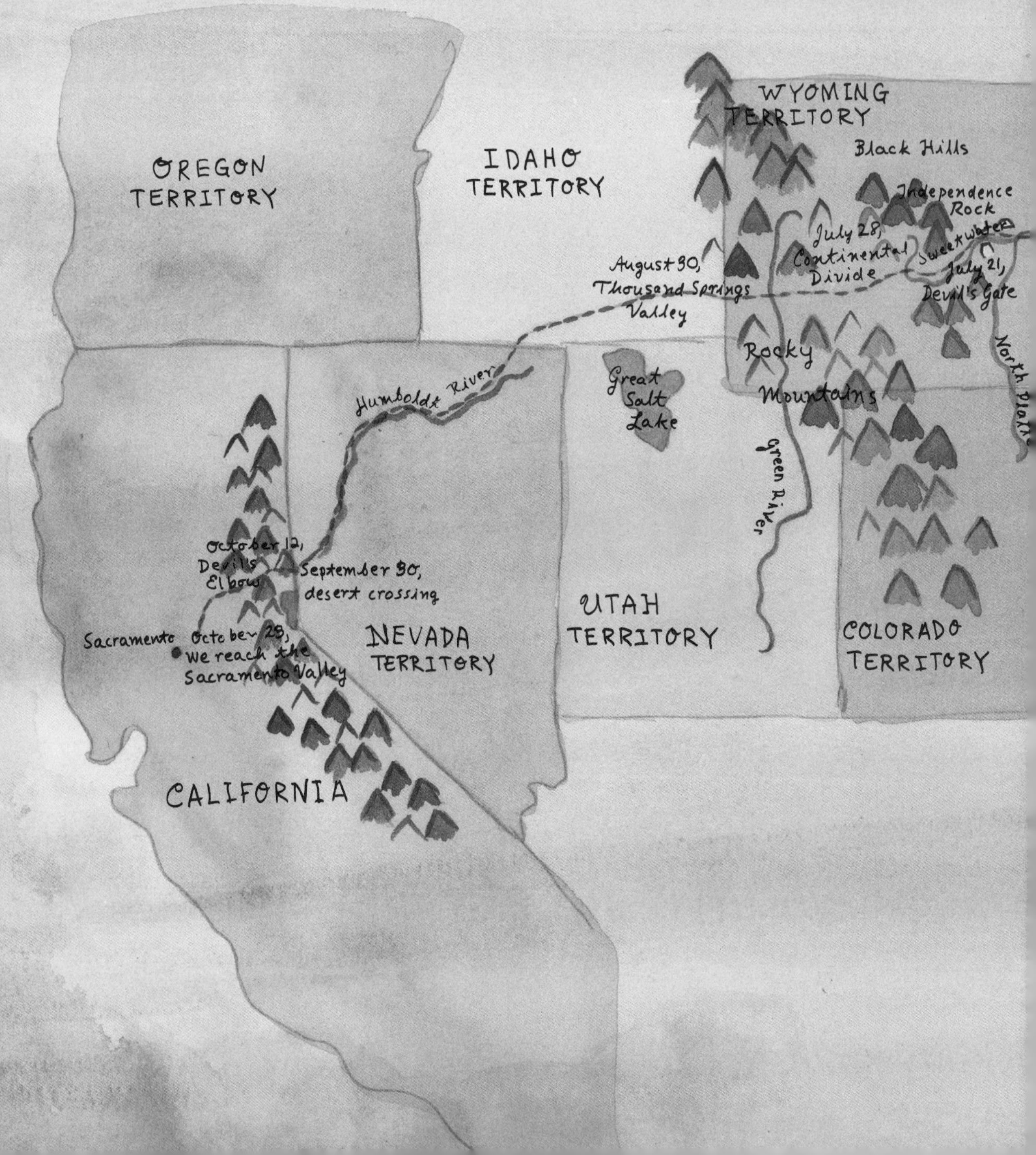
OREGON TERRITORY
IDAHO TERRITORY
WYOMING TERRITORY
Black Hills
Independence Rock
Sweetwater
July 21, Devil's Gate
July 28, Continental Divide
August 30, Thousand Springs Valley
North Platte
Rocky Mountains
Great Salt Lake
Green River
Humboldt River
October 12, Devil's Elbow
September 30, desert crossing
Sacramento
October 28, we reach the Sacramento Valley
NEVADA TERRITORY
UTAH TERRITORY
COLORADO TERRITORY
CALIFORNIA

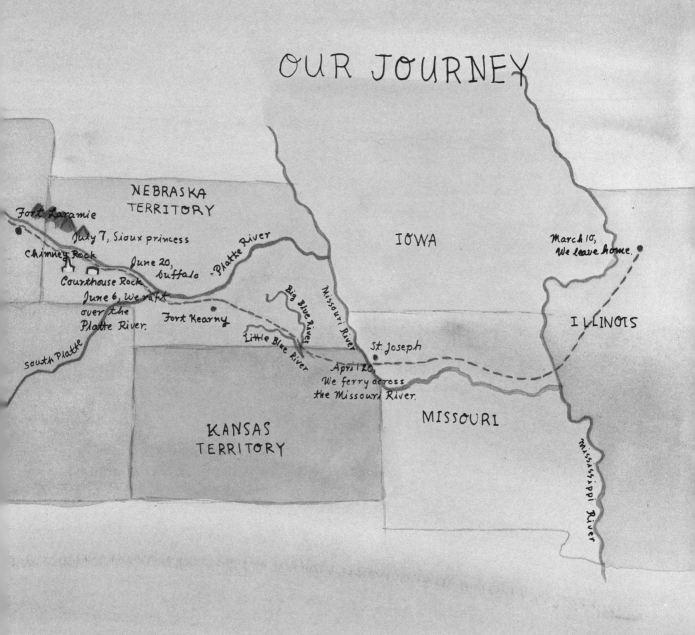

OUR JOURNEY

NEBRASKA TERRITORY

IOWA

March 10,
We leave home.

Fort Laramie

July 7, Sioux princess

Chimney Rock

Platte River

June 20,
buffalo

Courthouse Rock

June 6, We raft
over the
Platte River.

Fort Kearny

Missouri River

Big Blue River

ILLINOIS

Little Blue River

St. Joseph

April 20,
We ferry across
the Missouri River.

South Platte

MISSOURI

KANSAS TERRITORY

Mississippi River

Portable Iron Houses
RUST PROOF

The Galvanized Iron
Houses
Constructed by Me
for California
Eben Brown

J. G. Bridger

SOLE AGENT

"Domestic" Paper Fashions

"Hang sorrow. Care will kill a cat,
and therefore let us be merry."

THE STORY OF A PIONEER GIRL

Rachel's Journal

by
Marissa Moss

SCHOLASTIC INC.

New York Toronto London Auckland Sydney
Mexico City New Delhi Hong Kong

To Elias, who is always ready to
face hard work and adventure,

and with thanks to the Bancroft Library and especially
to Susan Snyder, librarian extraordinaire,
who helped me find much rich source material

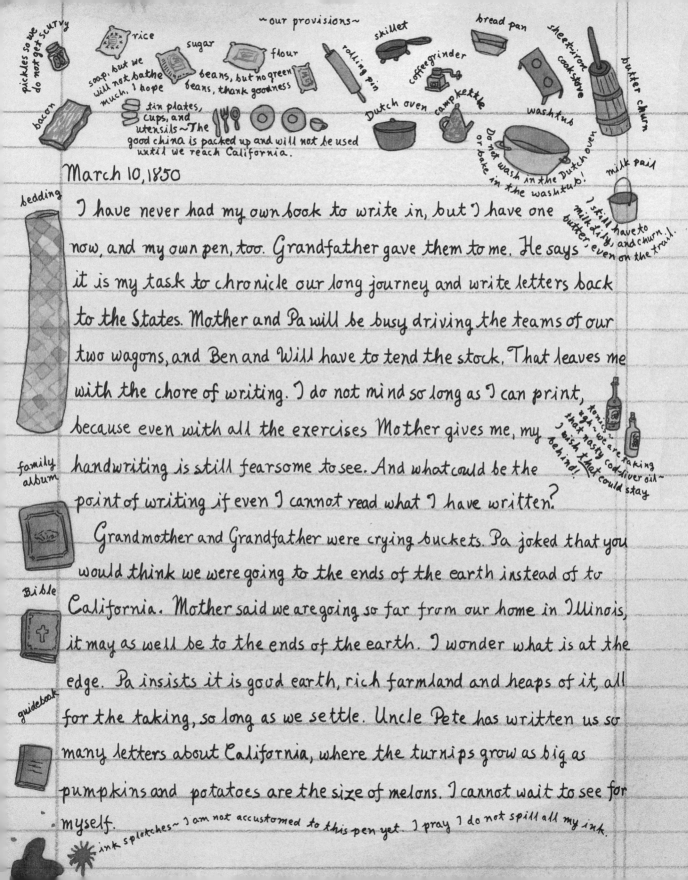

~our provisions~

pickles so we do not get scurvy

rice

sugar

soap, but we will not bathe much, I hope

flour

beans, but no green beans, thank goodness

bacon

skillet

bread pan

rolling pin

coffee grinder

sheet-iron cookstove

butter churn

tin plates, cups, and utensils ~ The good china is packed up and will not be used until we reach California.

Dutch oven

camp kettle

washtub

Do not wash in the Dutch oven or bake in the washtub!

milk pail

I still have to milk Lily, and churn butter, even on the trail.

March 10, 1850

bedding

I have never had my own book to write in, but I have one now, and my own pen, too. Grandfather gave them to me. He says it is my task to chronicle our long journey and write letters back to the States. Mother and Pa will be busy driving the teams of our two wagons, and Ben and Will have to tend the stock. That leaves me with the chore of writing. I do not mind so long as I can print, because even with all the exercises Mother gives me, my

tonics~ we are taking that nasty cod-liver oil~ I wish that could stay behind!

family album

handwriting is still fearsome to see. And what could be the point of writing if even I cannot read what I have written?

Bible

Grandmother and Grandfather were crying buckets. Pa joked that you would think we were going to the ends of the earth instead of to California. Mother said we are going so far from our home in Illinois, it may as well be to the ends of the earth. I wonder what is at the edge. Pa insists it is good earth, rich farmland and heaps of it, all

guidebook

for the taking, so long as we settle. Uncle Pete has written us so many letters about California, where the turnips grow as big as pumpkins and potatoes are the size of melons. I cannot wait to see for myself.

ink splotches~ I am not accustomed to this pen yet. I pray I do not spill all my ink.

Uncle Pete has described tall, tall trees and high snowy mountains. He says California is the most beautiful place in the world. We might even see a grizzly bear.

We all worked together to get the wagons ready. Ben and Will built a grub box to fit under the seat, while Mother and I sewed pockets into the wagon cover to hold small articles.

Pa had this picture taken before we left. Ben is 15 here, Will is 12, and I, Rachel, just turned 10. I am holding my cat, Biscuit, but Pa said I could not take her with, so I left her with my close friend, Millie Fremont. We will need a good mouser in California, but Pa said no.

~small articles~

needle

sewing pins

spyglass

looking glass

April 12, 1850

We have been on the road for more than a month, and we still have not left the States. I did not realize how big this country is! We have reached St. Joseph, Missouri, where we are to meet some neighbors to form a train together. I am sure I do not know how we will ever find them ~ white wagon covers stretch for miles. There are so many people and cattle waiting for the ferry to cross the Missouri River and start on the Oregon Trail, it seems our time will never come.

Pa says it is so crowded you cannot find a place to piss in peace. And it is even harder to find grass for our fifty head of cattle. We have to buy feed for them, an expense that makes Pa wince.

We brought the cattle because Pa says we can sell them for $20 ~ $50 a head in California. That is a fortune, so it is worth spending money on their feed now.

Independence Rock

Platte River

Chimney Rock

Courthouse Rock

Desert Scene

Devil's Gate

Prairie Wagon

Buffalo

Pa picked up this broadsheet in town to show us where we are going. I thought this would be an adventure, but I do not relish that desert scene. Ben says it is just meant to be dramatic, but dead cattle are not exciting to me.

Some days it seems I cannot even sew a button on ~ this one keeps coming off!

April 20, 1850

A week gone by, but we found everybody in that great milling throng and have been ferried across the wide and muddy Missouri. Mr. Elias was elected captain of our train, as he has been to California. Now he is going back with his family. There is another girl, 13 years old, named Prudence, but she strikes me as too full of herself to make a good friend. There are nine other children in our company, so I pray I will find someone to have adventures with. But I miss Millie ~ and Biscuit.

Mother is relieved that there are other women to talk with. She stays up late quilting around the fire. Pa teases her that she acts like this trip is one long quilting bee, but I can tell he likes to see her laughing with her friends. I try to quilt, too, but my stitches are as loose as my handwriting. Prudence is a natural wonder with needle and thread. Maybe the jolting wagon ride will make her fingers clumsy, maybe.

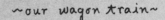

Captain John Elias

Mrs. Pamelia Elias ~ She is so short and round, she puts me in mind of a dumpling.

Prudence Elias ~ She has her own horse to ride and a sidesaddle. She is very proper, as Mother constantly reminds me. How I wish there were something she did badly!

Judith and Florence ~ 5-year-old twins ~ I cannot mark the difference between them, they are so like!

Asa ~ 2-years-old ~ He has golden curls like an angel and a sweet smile. He calls Prudence "Noodle," because that is the best he can say her name. I can think of other names that suit her better, but I cannot write them here.

Mrs. Arabella Sunshine ~ a long string bean of a woman

Almanzo ~ 10 years

Mr. James Sunshine

Frank ~ 6 years

Baby George ~ just turned 1 year

Caroline ~ 4 years

Emma ~ 7 years

Samuel ~ 12 years

Mr. Henry Sunshine ~ James's brother ~ He is not at all sunny but sour.

Mrs. Della Sunshine ~ his wife ~ She acts like a frightened mouse all the time. I think she is scared of Mr. Henry Sunshine.

Mrs. Louisa Sunshine   Mr. Hugh Sunshine ~ their son

Mr. Bridger ~ He has the longest whiskers I ever saw, probably to make up for the distinct lack of hair on top of his head.

Jesse   Daniel   John   Jim   Lee

Vigor   Valor

our two lead oxen ~ They seem like part of the family to me.

The 5 bachelors are on their way to the gold mines. They are helping drive the stock in exchange for cooking by the Sunshine women. Between all the wagons, we have 115 head of cattle and oxen.

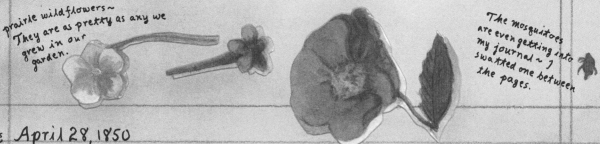

prairie wildflowers~ They are as pretty as any we grew in our garden.

The mosquitoes into my journal~ I swatted one between the pages.

April 28, 1850

The wide expanse of the Great Plains is now before us. As far as we can see, there is tall grass all around, dotted with beautiful wildflowers. At first the other wagon trains were so thick about us, we saw more of schooner "sails" than of the prairie. Now the crowds have thinned out, and when we camped for the night we felt truly alone, like small specks in a vast ocean of wilderness. I ached for home for the first time, but Ben played his fiddle while Mother sang, and that cheered us all.

The mosquitoes here are as big as flies and just as common. I hate them!

May 3, 1850

I am used to bumping around in the wagon (Pa says I have got my sea legs), but I cannot get used to the mosquitoes. One leg is swollen up and I have a horrid bump over my eye. Prudence has it worse, though. She has a bright red bite on her nose.

The jolting ride spares me the chore of churning butter, but I still have to collect fuel for the fire each night. Yesterday there was no wood to be found. Mrs. Sunshine suggested that we twist grasses together into coils and burn that. Mr. Elias laughed and said there was plenty of fuel all around us, lying almost at

How to make butter on the trail: After milking the cow in the morning, put the cream in the churn, which is tied to the back of the wagon. By evening the rutted road will have churned the butter for you.

Prudence is always looking in the glass to admire her fresh sunbonnet and curls. (Even here she puts her hair in papers for the night.) But not anymore~ who wants to admire a pustule on the tip of their nose?

Ben jokes that next we will cook with rat droppings.

cozy campfire

beans and rice with buffalo spice

Riddle: When is a muffin not a muffin?

When it is a buffalo chip!

Even a spoonful of jam will not improve that muffin's flavor!

our feet. I could not see at all what he meant, but then he picked up a buffalo chip and lit it. Now I gather "meadow muffins." It takes quite a pile of them for a lasting fire, but at least they are light and easy to find.

Prudence declares it is one thing to gather them (which she grudgingly does), but another to eat anything cooked with them ~ the thought of supper smoked in buffalo droppings curdles her milk. I think they make a fine fuel, and they do not smell at all (so long as they are good and dry. I surely would not pick up a wet one!) So I was content to feast on beans and rice. I smacked my lips loudly, praising the delicious meal, but Prudence turned away and went to bed, too fine for such coarse fare.

May 5, 1850

Today I discovered another use for meadow muffins. If you light one and place it in the wagon, as it smolders the smoke drives away the mosquitoes. An additional benefit is that the smoke also keeps Prudence away. She has taken to spending evenings with us ~ surely not on my behalf. She is too busy fluttering her eyelashes at Ben. That is sickening enough to drive me away.

Prudence's delicate nose held high in the air, away from the fumes. She bats her eyes at Ben while she picks at her food ~ she gave in to eating after only one day.

Ben making cow eyes back at Prudence ~ that is a sight to make you lose your appetite!

Will declares buffalo chips better than balls. He, Ben, Almanzo, and Samuel toss them around or pelt each other with them like snowballs. I wish I could join them, but Mother says I am not to be a wild ruffian. It is so much more diverting to be a ruffian.

cut~off path

berry bushes

little stream

shade

May 10, 1850

Pa says we are taking the Oregon Trail until it splits and we veer south for California. Now we are following the Platte River. The sight of the broad river and the bluffs is restful, but the dust kicked up by all the stock is not. Especially when our wagons are in the rear ~ then it is so thick, I can barely see past our own teams. But I found a way to escape the heat and dirt of the main road. All along the trail there are narrow cut~off paths. Pa says they were made and used by Indians and hunters. These cut~offs run diagonally to the road and are often by shady creeks, so they are pleasant to walk along. Since they always lead back to the trail, there is no need to fret about getting lost. The boys have to drive the stock, so they have no choice but to eat dust, but I take the younger children with me, and we have great fun, picking berries and wildflowers and wading in the creeks.

These berries were a little sour.

These berries were sour if you ate them when they were red, but delicious if you ate them when they were black.

May 16, 1850

Today I had my first adventure. We had been walking on the cut~off for 2~3 hours, traveling upstream into a deep canyon. The trail was not only out of sight, but out of earshot as well. I liked feeling alone, but Emma fretted that we were lost and the twins were tired, whining that a jouncing wagon ride would be better than tramping on. I tried

to cheer everyone by singing "Turkey in the Straw" when we heard a rustling in the bushes. Something much larger than a turkey ~ Indians! Frank pulled out his little knife, all fierceness, but I hushed him and went to look for myself. (All quaking inside, I admit, but I could not let _them_ see that!) And what should I see when I parted the bushes with trembling hand? The moist snout of a very content ox, chomping on leaves. Somebody must have lost him. If it _had_ been an Indian, Frank declared, he would have protected us. I hope we have no such need.

That was just the beginning of our adventure. When the cut~off reached the trail, there was no sign of our train, either ahead or behind. There was nothing for it but to continue on the cut~off in the hopes of coming out ahead of our wagons soon. On and on we walked. Frank and Emma never complained, nor did little Caroline, but those twins whined worse than the mosquitoes. Still we found no wagons. The sun set, the buffalo wolves started in to howl, and it was too dark to see the trail before us. I would have sat down in the darkness and cried, but I had to take care of the others. Then I recalled what Ben had said about looking for a high view point if you get lost, so I urged everyone up a hill before us. It was not very high, but we were rewarded with the sight of 3 campfires. Since our train is not large, we headed for the smallest one, going straight

Wherever there are buffalo, there are wolves.

We pass many graves, like these, but the markers never say anyone was killed by Indians. Instead they say drowning, lightning, mountain fever, or cholera. Cholera is the worst!

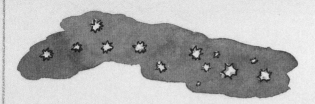

The stars were beautiful, but I was too fretful to enjoy them until we got home ~ then they seemed to be laughing at me.

across country. We barged through brambles and sloshed through creeks, but we always kept that light in view, like the beacon of a lighthouse.

At last I was greeted with the welcome sight of Prudence nibbling bacon. I could not help but embrace her, though she did not appreciate my smudged arms and dress. In fact, she was so startled by our abrupt appearance, she screamed as if we were ghosts or Indians.

The bacon and coffee smelled wonderful!

Mrs. Arabella Sunshine, Mrs. Elias, and Mother were first joyous, then mad. In between hugging me and scrubbing my face, Mother scolded. Now I cannot take cut~offs after the noon break. That means swallowing dust in the hottest part of the day. At least we still have the mornings.

May 23, 1850

Now we are not permitted ever to walk along the cut~offs! Not that we got lost today ~ something much more exciting happened. Once again we were out of sight of the train, singing as we strolled, when an Indian brave came riding straight at us. I was so amazed to see a true Indian, I forgot to be frightened. We all stood staring at him (though Frank once again reached for his knife ~ I hissed at him to leave it be, no sense asking for trouble). The twins hid behind my skirt, and the others huddled around me when the brave rode up to us and leapt off his pony. You could have heard a pin drop! He stepped toward me

hair, long and braided like a girl's

feathers

bow, arrows and quiver

buckskin breeches with fringe (his only clothes!)

beaded moccasins

Indian hand

my hand

I wish I could draw him better. He was very handsome, with smooth coppery skin and dark hair and eyes. He rode bareback on a spotted pony.

and said something, then held his hand straight out. I did not know what else to do, but shake it, so I did. And that was exactly what he wanted! He offered his hand to each child. Even Frank shook it, grinning so broadly his mouth looked like he had swallowed an ear of corn whole.

The brave knew some English, and he clearly thought we were lost. He asked if I knew where our wagon was. I nodded yes. Satisfied that we were not in trouble, he got back on his pony, waved good-bye, and rode off. It was all over in two shakes of a lamb's tail. After all the horrible stories we had heard about Indians, we had a story of our own to tell and a pretty funny one at that. Only somehow when the adults heard of our meeting, they were not amused. Instead they lectured us on all the awful things that <u>might</u> have happened. And so the cut-offs are forbidden from now on.

Frank grinning

May 30, 1850

It has rained for days, which has the benefit of keeping down the dust but the disadvantage of turning the trail into an enormous puddle. Despite our cover claiming to be watertight, everything is soaked through. The Platte is swollen and wild. I am relieved we do

My shoes are so caked with mud, they are more mud pie than footwear.

Sunbonnets are definitely not meant for rain, unless you find a sopping curtain before your face desirable ~ I do not!

It is hard keeping this journal dry ~ I do my best.

not have to ford it. Pa says we will reach the government ferry tomorrow.

June 7, 1850

Yesterday was the first time I truly felt scared. Getting lost, howling wolves, Indians ~ nothing compares to the fury of this river! We arrived at the ferry only to discover that it had broken loose of its moorings when the rains started. Some men finally retrieved it, but it took so long that an enormous line of wagons waited ahead of us to take the ferry. The man said it would be 3 weeks before our turn came. Mr. Elias warned that we were already behind schedule and such a long delay would surely mean crossing the Sierra Nevada Mountains in the snow. No one wants to suffer the fate of the Donner Party, frozen and starving in the mountains. Mr. Elias determined that we should take the wagons off their wheel beds and raft them over the river. The current was swift and the banks like quicksand, but there was no other way. Both Sunshine families balked at the danger and refused to go first. Mr. Elias offered to cross, but he has young children, so Pa suggested we go. Mother's face was drawn tight, but she nodded. Ben and Will stayed behind to drive the stock over, so Pa, Mother, and I each took a pole to make our way across. The waves were high and it was hard to keep from tipping. Twice I almost fell in. The second time I

Another bad thing about rain ~ it is too wet to cook, so all we eat are cold biscuits that lodge in my craw like a lump of clay. Oh, for some of grandmother's hot lamb stew!

Mr. Bridger should have gone first, but he never does anything for anyone ~ he is the most selfish man I ever laid eyes on!

Ben loves to tell the story of the Donner Party to frighten the little ones. I confess, it chills me. Four years ago, the Donners and some others took a "shortcut" that put them in the Sierras when the snows started. Worse yet, most of those who lived survived by eating their dead companions' flesh ~ ugh! Some of them starved to death.

The worst part was trying to avoid the sandy islands in the middle of the broad river.

We lashed the two wagons together and piled all our provisions on, covered with an india rubber sheet.

I could not steer worth a bean.

Prudence bit her lips so hard during the crossing, she drew blood, but I admit, she did her share of work.

Lazy Mr. Bridger hired Lee and Jim to ferry him and his wagon across, leaving fewer men to help with the stock.

lost my pole and clung on to the wagon hoops, not much help to anyone after that. Somehow we landed. My knuckles were white from holding so tightly to the hoops, but Mother's face was even paler. What a relief to be on land again!

The others followed with no mishap. (And Frank declared that he was not scared, not a bit. I do not credit that!) Only the stock still had to be driven over. Ben and Will, along with Samuel, John, Daniel, and Jesse, rounded up all 115 head of cattle and drove them to the river, but they refused to go in. They had no idea of the dangers of the Sierras, but they could plainly see the dangers of the Platte. Three times the boys gathered the cattle together only to have them split and stampede at the water's edge. It was getting dark, and it looked like we would have to camp on opposite shores when Will decided he had stood enough, he would make those cattle cross. He rode next to Bo, the lead herd ox, and just as the stubborn animal reached the banks, Will leapt from his horse onto Bo's back, clung to his horns, and, kicking and screaming, drove that ox into the river. And it worked! Bo started swimming across and all the stock followed. Safe on the other side, Will jumped off Bo and looked back to see his own horse foundering in the water. His foreleg had gotten tangled up in the loose reins. Will rushed into the water to free his horse just as a clap of thunder split the sky open. Lightning flashed with an eerie brightness followed by pitch black and the deafening roll of thunder.

In the dark we could not see Will, but his horse clambered safely onto shore. When the next lightning flashed, Pa cried out that Will had made it to a sandbar in the river. Whether he was dead or alive, no one could say, and while the storm raged, no one dared swim out to rescue him.

That was a miserable and awful night! It was total confusion~ thunder booming, oxen bellowing, children crying, men shouting, as light as day one minute, as dark as a cave the next. Add to that the torment of not knowing how poor Will fared and feeling utterly helpless to do anything for him. All we could do was huddle together, a pile of drenched human rags, as the men worked blindly to control the stock.

At dawn the storm quieted, and Pa rushed into the churning river and brought back Will's limp body. He was so pale and still, I thought sure he was dead. Pa started rubbing him down with whiskey, trickling it down his throat. At first it ran out the corners of his mouth. Then I saw him swallow! When at last he opened his eyes, the

I never thought I would be so happy to see the sun rise.

...tried to use this time to write letters home, but although so much has happened, ...do not know what to say. That life is so far away ~ sleeping in beds, petting Biscuit, ...aving friends and family nearby (but not as close together as we all are here ~ you cannot ...neeze without a chorus of "bless you"). Will I ever have a real home again?

...whole company cheered. He was alive! I have never been so proud ~ nor so scared.

June 15, 1850

We took some days' rest to wash everything and dry it out, to put the wagons back together and repair them, to coddle Will and return him to his usual good health. We are fortunate no one drowned in that crossing. There are several new graves of men who died that way, and we heard that in a wagon train near ours, a woman was killed by lightning. Will has always claimed to live a charmed life, and now I believe him.

June 20, 1850

A different kind of storm passed by us today ~ a herd of buffalo. It was as if the river had leapt out of its banks and taken solid form to chase us down. A thick cloud of dust surged toward us, then there was a tremendous noise, an earthly thunder. We could see their shaggy backs rising and falling like a great wave. Nothing could turn back such a force, so we hastily pulled the wagons close together while the boys drove the stock away ~ for once a cow or an ox is caught up in a buffalo stampede, it is gone for good, part of a new wild herd.

I try to remember Millie, but I can scarce call up her face. Grandmother and Grandfather are clearer. How I wish I could roast chestnuts with them now! I wonder if they still think on us, as I think on them, missing them.

deer tracks

buffalo tracks

spuoy

We cowered in the wagons and watched them come closer and closer. Mother tried to keep me back, but I wanted to see them as best I could. After all, if they plowed into us I would not be any safer in the middle of the wagon than in the front. So I poked my head out into the whirling dust storm. I could see their rolling eyes and flaring nostrils, but Will must have brought us some of his charmed luck, and the massive beasts thundered by and not _through_ us. I have seen cattle stampede, but this was different — buffalo are so big and so wild. I wished I could run after them.

Of course, I could not. But Pa and Mr. Elias did, eager to hunt the famous beasts. Mother, meantime, insisted we all bathe in the river as we were cloaked in dust. Not very thrilling, but it did feel good to be clean, at least for a while.

We baked bread and dried-apple pies, and had a fine feast when Pa and Mr. Elias returned with the meat of a young bull. Our first fresh meat in months! And it was every bit as good as Grandmother's roast.

The leftover meat we jerked and hung on strings to dry, fluttering in the wind like festive red flags.

Sometimes we pass buffalo heads that emigrants have cut off and used as stools. (But don't sit on those horns!)

Frank ran around pretending to be a buffalo while Emma and I hunted him.

barely used soap (I am so accustomed now to cold river water, I can scarce recall what a warm bath feels like. Prudence, howsomever, never ceases to bewail the lack of hot water.)

~embroidery square~

I am not such a fine hand at stitching as Prudence, but I have learned how to make whips and drive the team, and she has not.

June 25, 1850

We are all used to traveling together now, and for the most part we get along fine (even Prudence and me). The two Sunshine brothers constantly argue, but only with each other, so we pay them no mind. Pa still finds Mr. Bridger's laziness galling, but he is very fond of Mr. Elias. Mrs. Elias, Mrs. Arabella Sunshine, and Mother gossip together and exchange recipes, dreaming of the days when they can really cook again. Will and Ben are fast friends with Samuel and Almanzo, and the four often play cards (when they tire of tossing buffalo chips). As for me, I like to ride with Emma. Quilting and embroidery are more bearable if you have company. (Though it does not improve my work, it improves my mood.)

Mother tries to school us still. We just finished _King Lear_ and the description of the storm put me in mind of our own Platte River thunderstorm. The Bible seems even more apt, as we have just started Exodus, our own as well as the biblical one. Pa says we are going to our own promised land of milk and honey. Amen, Mother says. Ben jokes that he hopes we do not wander 40 years in the desert like the Hebrews did. Looking back at the desert scene in the broadsheet, I shudder at the thought.

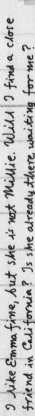

I like Emma fine, but she is not Millie. Will I find a close friend in California? Is she already there, waiting for me?

Niger   Valor

The road has been very sandy, and the wagons are so heavy they sink in sand up to the hubs. It is tough going, especially for the lead oxen.

June 28, 1850

The grass has been thin for days now, as all the many emigrants before us have eaten it up. (I mean, *they* have not, but their cattle have.) Last night Valor was so hungry, he started rooting in the wagon for feed. Luckily he did not get into our provisions, but he made a nice meal of my one wool dress. He also chewed up part of the friendship quilt our folks gave us when we left Illinois. I am not sure which loss devastated Mother more. She saved what quilt blocks she could, but there was not much more than a pocket left of the dress. Rather than risk my good cotton dress (now well hidden), I am wearing Will's other shirt and britches, along with my sunbonnet, of course. Mother is not pleased with me turning into a boy, and Prudence lords her own frills over me more than ever, but I do not care, not much. At least now it will be easier to gather wild currants and berries. Nor will the wind whip my skirt in my face anymore. (Though Prudence will never admit to it, I know that she and the 3 Mrs. Sunshines have sewn rocks into the hems to keep their dresses down. They may be spared the embarrassment of revealing their underthings, but their shins are black and blue from the constant banging of rocks against them.)

suspicious lumps in their skirts

splotchy bruises on their legs

Grandmother's quilt block

Aunt Winifred's quilt block

At least Vader had the good sense to eat the plainest parts of the quilt.

July 1, 1850

Today we passed an Indian grave, the first after so many, many emigrant graves. The body was wrapped in a blanket set up on a platform in a tree's branches. I would have thought this a curious method of burial, but having seen so many trailside graves dug up by wolves, it seems very sensible.

There were some beads (from the dead person's clothes? the blanket?) scattered on the ground, and Emma, Frank, and I raced to collect as many as we could. Frank was eager to show his treasure to Caroline and Baby George. (Not that George would have much of a response other than to try to eat them, as he does everything within reach ~ he once shoved a buffalo chip into his mouth and Emma had to pry it out.) Frank was so impatient, he tried to climb into the wagon as it was moving. We have all done so hundreds of times with no mishap, but this time Frank fell

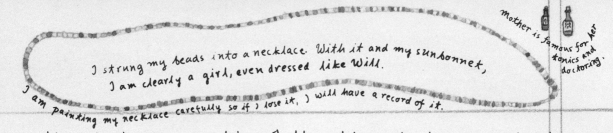

I strung my beads into a necklace. With it and my sunbonnet, I am clearly a girl, even dressed like Will.

I am painting my necklace carefully so if I lose it, I will have a record of it.

Mother is famous for her tonics and doctoring.

and the wheels ran over him. I thought surely he was crushed to death, but only his leg was broken. His face was white, but he did not cry when Mother set and bandaged his leg. (I think the whiskey helped.) The first thing he said was "What about my beads?" so of course we collected the fallen beads for him. Now he is stuck in the jolting wagon for the rest of the trip, but I promised him anything interesting that I find, and to ease the boredom I gave him our spyglass to use and appointed him our lookout.

Will tried to cheer Frank up by baking fresh bread for supper, but he forgot to sift the flour, so the dough was peppered with mouse "pills." No one was hungry enough to eat that, but we had a good laugh, Frank loudest of all.

These are not raisins! It is one thing to cook with buffalo droppings. It is another to eat mouse droppings. No, thank you!

The bread was only fit for a mouse to nibble.

July 4, 1850

We finally came to the first landmark on the broadsheet ~ Courthouse Rock. It looked so close, Mother allowed us to ride out so that we could add our names to it, as many others come before us have. Even Prudence wanted to go. But instead of a couple of hours, it took the rest of the day to reach it ~ the prairie gives the illusion of small distances as there is nothing to

Keturah Wilde   OSCAR BELNAP   Prudence Elids

We used Frank's knife to carve all
our names into the rock's soft surface
(Frank's name first, as I promised).
So many people have been here.
I loved reading the names and
becoming part of the
roster.

Ben gallantly carved Prudence's
name next to his own~ how
she beamed up at him!

provide a sense of scale. Having come so far, however, we were determined
not to return until we had climbed that rock. My britches proved
an advantage, and I was the only girl to make it to the top. Ben, Will,
Samuel, Almanzo, and I viewed the sunset from on high. It was glorious!
We galloped back in the dark, but the moon was full and the campfire
was clear before us. Racing across that broad expanse, tasting the
crisp night air, with so many stars twinkling above us and the moon's
silvery light casting purple shadows before us, I felt like I was a
hawk soaring. I did not want to stop, ever.

But when we reached the wagons, we found everybody celebrating~
dancing, singing, speechifying. We had forgotten that it was
Independence Day! A real feast greeted our sharpened appetites.
There were dishes we had not tasted in months. Frank was chin deep
into a cherry pie. Cherries! Mrs. Arabella Sunshine had saved canned fruit
for the celebration. Everyone contributed something.

I was too excited to sleep, so I just looked up at the stars thinking
how odd it was to celebrate America's birthday when we were leaving the
United States. If we love our country so much, why are we
going so far away?

ham

fresh picked wild onions~
vegetables taste delicious when
you have not eaten any in months.

sausages

pickles

cheese

Praise Lily, the milk cow!

butter

bread (without mice spice)

fruit pies (canned, not dried)

biscuits

fruitcake Mother baked in
Illinois and saved for
today

I found some beautiful rocks along the trail. I just had to keep them, though Mother scolded me for weighing down the poor oxen so needlessly.

They are only 3 small rocks—what harm can they do?

July 5, 1850

Pa says we are not leaving the States, we are going to Opportunity. Besides, California will be a state someday, now that we have won the war with Mexico. Mother says not to count on that. But there is already a provisional American government in California, with a governor in charge, so I agree with Pa.

The squaws lead the ponies. The braves ride ahead. Ponies have poles fastened to them and everything is loaded onto them—even babies in cradle boards! Dogs carry baggage the same way.

baby in board

July 7, 1850

I wanted to climb Chimney Rock when we came to it today, but passing between us and it was a large train of Sioux, moving their entire village. The chief and his daughter rode over to visit with us. The girl looked like a princess, and we could see how proud the old chief was of her. Ben gave her biscuits and sugar (until Prudence glared icily at him). I wanted to give her something, too, something that would last, not be eaten and forgotten. I begged Mother to let me give her a small looking glass, and when I did, she gave me such a sunny smile, I see it still, hours later. She let me pet her pony and showed us the tricks she could do riding it. Even Frank

She wore a loose white buckskin gown, soft as silk.

Ben had a lot of fawning to do over Prudence to make up for the smiles he gave the princess.

He picked a bouquet of wildflowers as a peace token.

fell in love with her. He offered her his treasured knife! She took it, waved her hand, and was gone, like a rainbow vanishes after a shower. I did not climb Chimney Rock, but I will have wonderful dreams tonight, galloping on my own pony next to the princess.

July 12, 1850

While we were at supper a boy walked into camp. Like the Sioux, he had all his belongings with him, loaded onto a cow. His name is Simon, and he walked all the way from Ohio by himself. Sometimes he camped with nearby emigrants, but mostly he has been alone. Mother was horrified that one so young should be by himself in this great wilderness ~ he cannot be more than 12. Of course, we fed him supper (which he bolted like a famished dog), and after some hurried whispers from Mother to Pa, and from Pa to Mr. Bridger, Mr. Bridger invited Simon to join his wagon. Simon can drive the team in exchange for his food. Simon does not smile much, but I think he is glad of the company. Mr. Bridger, naturally, is delighted ~ one fewer task to keep him from napping.

Mr. Bridger as we usually find him, snoring before the campfire

He loves to toast his fragrant feet~ something the rest of us do not at all relish. The only thing worse than his rank socks are his warm rank socks!

Hold stock firmly in both hands, circle lash 2-3 times over oxen's heads, then with a quick forward movement, crack the whip ~ but take care, if the cracker hits you, it hurts like the dickens!

stock

braided lash

cracker

How to make a whip (you need new ones every so often because the old ones wear down until they are useless stubs): 1. Cut down a sapling 6-8 feet long, trim off limbs (this is the stock). 2. Make a braided lash 6-10 feet long with a good buckskin cracker. 3. Tie lash securely to stock.

July 17, 1850

Simon has proven to be a wonderful addition to our company. It took him a while to learn to crack the whip. (On his first try, the lash went in the opposite direction intended and peeled the skin off the top of his nose.) Now he is an expert. He whips the oxen until their noses almost touch the back of the wagon ahead, then he climbs into the wagon and brings out his fiddle. By the time he jumps to the ground again, the oxen are already lagging, so while he tunes the fiddle with his fingers, he kicks the oxen with his feet. Between lashes, he plays short tunes, like "Buffalo Gals." Not exactly music to soothe the weary oxen, more likely to rend a rock or split a cabbage, but the rest of us find it merry. Evenings, Simon and Ben play together and we all sing along. That is the best part of the day, when we are gathered together by the campfire. Then home does not seem as far away.

30 stars for 30 states

We posted letters at Fort Laramie. The flag points west because someday all the land west of here will be part of the United States. Pa says the eagle points west because someday there looks like this.

Friendly fiddles

July 21, 1850

We have left the Platte and are now following the Sweetwater River. I have not been recording our passage as faithfully as I

rocks | Devil's Gate | rocks

Sweetwater River

Devil's Gate is not really a gate ~ it is ridges of steep cliffs through which the river passes. Emma and I climbed the cliffs and crawled out to the edge. The sheer drop was dizzying! We could hear the river roaring below, though we were so high it looked like a silver thread. In the distance was our first view of the Rocky Mountains.

~chores~
milk the cow
bake bread
clean dishes
wash clothes
gather fuel
quilt
embroider
practice sums

Danger

Poison

should. Despite what Grandfather said, I _do_ have work to do. Anyway, at this late date, I should note that we have passed Independence Rock and Devil's Gate and are traveling through the Black Hills. The views are pretty, but I miss the wide~open space of the prairie.

Ezra Stone died from cholera

July 24, 1850

Early in the trip, we took care to read each marker and give the dead a moment of prayer, but if we kept that up, we would still be in Nebraska!

We are so slow with all the stock we have to feed and water that usually other wagons pass us by, but today we overtook a large train that had stopped because several people were sick with cholera. Eight had already died from it. I am sure we passed their graves, but we pass _so_ many graves, I have almost stopped seeing them ~ they are just a part of the landscape.

Mr. Elias rushed us past the sad settlement, and we all held our breaths, hoping to escape contagion. Mr. Henry Sunshine had a fever once and Baby George had flux for a week, but we have been very healthy. Perhaps that revolting tonic works after all.

July 28, 1850

I knew we were higher, as it had gotten much colder, but I was still surprised to learn we had crossed the pass of the Rocky Mountains, the ascent had been so gentle and gradual. When we came to the Continental Divide, we celebrated with a noon treat of strawberries

Another danger is alkali poisoning. Patches of white powder are all over the ground, and they sometimes crust up watering holes. Once an animal drinks that water, it is bound to die, and it is hard work keeping the stock away.

Mother doubled the dose of Dr. Dibble's bitters today. I have never tasted anything beastlier, but I do not want to sicken.

Pacific Springs flows west.

The Continental Divide
lies in between ~
you can feel the force of
this invisible line.

A few paces away another stream
flows east.

and cream, but my heart felt sad. This was our final good-bye to our family back east. We have passed an important boundary, and I wonder if I will ever see my grandparents again. From now on, all rivers and streams flow west, as if pulling us with them. There is no turning back.

   Where we camped, there was another important marker ~ snow! Snow in July! Perhaps not a lot, but still there it was. Will did not believe me when I told him about it, so I gave him proof ~ a fine, fat snowball smack on his neck! That started a snowball fight. Even Prudence could not resist. (So she, too, is sometimes a ruffian!) She nicked my ear, but I landed a good one right in her face. Poor Frank wanted so badly to join us, he hobbled around as best he could. But he missed Emma completely and hit an ox. (I was hoping for

Mr. Bridger.)

It is a wonder to see strawberries growing despite the chill.

I cannot reckon who was more astonished, Prudence or the ox.

We all sat around the campfire to dry out, cheered by the frolic. (Except for the ox, that is.)

July 30, 1850
Several cows strayed during the night, so the men went out to search

Mr. Bridger, asleep and without a gun.

loosened belt

for them. (Except, of course, for lazy Mr. Bridger, who decided the late start was a good excuse for a nap.) Will was so disgusted by Mr. Bridger's sloth that before he left, he loosened the sleeping man's belt, took off his pistol, and hid it. I hoped that snoring beauty would not awake until Will returned, so he could enjoy the effects of his trick. Mr. Bridger woke up much before then, but the joke went even better than Will intended.

A small group of Indians rode into our camp, waking Mr. Bridger, who heroically leapt to his feet, reaching for his gun. Not only did he miss the pistol, his britches started to fall down! While he frantically fastened his belt and searched for his gun, Mother and Mrs. Elias approached the Indians. Mother did not know whether to be stern and fierce or friendly, but Mrs. Elias assured her that since they wore no war paint, there was nothing to fear. Still it was a worrisome sight ~ such big, strange men in our midst. They must have understood our qualms, for they dismounted and smiled. They called themselves Pawnees and eagerly accepted the biscuits we hurriedly offered. True enough, they were not warlike, but they did poke their noses into everything. (They were especially curious about Mrs. Della Sunshine's corset hanging out to dry. One brave tried it

"Speak!" ~ extend the open hand from the chin.
"I am angry!" ~ close the fist, place it against the forehead and twist it to and fro against the forehead.

Our guidebook says to use these gestures to talk to Indians, but they did not seem to understand any of them.

I hoped for a dress like the Sioux princess wore. Maybe the next Indians we meet will have one to trade.

my beautiful moccasins~ buckskin with a piece of scarlet broadcloth edged with beads

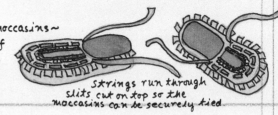

Strings run through slits cut on top so the moccasins can be securely tied

on his head as a bonnet. I could not help but laugh, though Mother glared at me and poor Mrs. Sunshine turned red as a beet.)

Mother traded some sugar for some moccasins for me, and Emma's mother bartered flour for a pair for Emma. But when all the trading was done, the Pawnees did not seem ready to leave. The 3 Mrs. Sunshines grew more and more fretful. Prudence clutched Asa so tightly, he started to wail. Meanwhile, Mr. Bridger was tearing through his provisions, swearing to shame a goat, still looking for that "where in tarnation" gun. I am sure the Pawnees thought him crazy.

Then, on some impulse she never could explain, Mrs. Louisa Sunshine dropped out her false teeth. I suppose it was nerves, but to the Pawnees, it was devils' work. They rushed off, screaming. (I must confess, her wrinkled, toothless gums were a fearsome sight.) So the hero of the day was not Mr. Bridger, but Mrs. Sunshine and her teeth. When the men returned (and Will led Mr. Bridger to his hidden gun), it was   no teeth here

hard to tell who laughed more at our story~

Will or sour Mr. Sunshine!

August 3, 1850

We took the Sublette cut~off to avoid Salt

Mrs. Louisa Sunshine

teeth here!

TOM RICHARDS WENT TO CAL NOT TO OREGON

SPENGLER PARTY TOOK HUDSPETH CUT-OFF

← WATER

GOOD GRASS →

The guide book tells of deserts, rivers, mountains, cut-offs, even Indian smoke language, but it does not indicate bad water.

Lake City. Since then, the roads have been steep and rocky. This last day took us through a patch of desert, with neither water nor grass for the stock. Mr. Henry Sunshine was leading (we take turns, as those in front swallow much less dust than those in the rear), and came to the first spring of water in many hours. The lead oxen lunged for the water and started to drink. Mr. Sunshine was unyoking the rest of his team, all bellowing madly with thirst, when Mr. Elias, in the second wagon, noticed a sign on a piece of wood trampled in the dirt. It read POISON! DO NOT DRINK! FRESH WATER THAT WAY—→.

Mr. Sunshine drove out his oxen in a panic, but it was too late for the lead pair. He dosed them with bacon and gunpowder, but they started bleeding from the nose and were dead within hours. We were lucky no one else had drunk of that terrible water! What if Mr. Elias had not seen the sign? What if no one had written it to warn us?

Another stretch of desert lies before us, so we camped early by the freshwater to allow the stock to feed and rest up. We are low on provisions, so the boys went hunting with the 3 Mr. Sunshines while the women washed, baked, and cooked. Pa and Mr. Elias repaired the wagons and shoed the stock. Mr. Bridger, naturally, slept ~ only this time he used his pistol as a pillow, so as not to lose it again.

I wished I could go hunting with Ben and Will, but I did not dare ask Mother. She frets enough that I am losing ladylike graces. The farther we get from the States, the more "uncivilized" she finds me. I am not the ruffian she thinks, but it is hard to be a lady on the dusty trail, and hunting is much more exciting than washing clothes. But I washed clothes.

And for once I was content to stay behind washing, because although we did not go on an adventure, an adventure came to us. Into our scene of domestic chores rode a war party of about 60 Pawnees. They were upon us before we knew it, and even if prepared, what could we have done? There were so few of us and so many of them. We all just froze where we were, sure that it had come at last ~ the dreaded massacre.

But despite the war paint, the Pawnees made no threatening moves or cries. An old warrior, the chief I guessed, dismounted and spoke to us in English. They were on the warpath, as we thought, but against the Sioux, not against the whites. What they wanted from us were the 2 dead oxen. Mr. Elias tried to make the chief understand that the meat was poisoned, but he insisted, so we gave them the carcasses.

At once, several Indians set to cutting up the oxen. The more

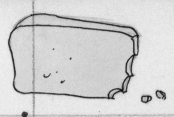

One Pawnee tried a piece of cheese. He acted like it was cod-liver oil and spat it out, crinkling up his nose. Was this dog food or people food, he wanted to know. I reckon we eat what they give their dogs!

curious ones came into our camp, asking to taste our cooking. One brave was fascinated by my freckles. Thinking they were some kind of war paint, he reached a finger out and tried to rub the "paint" off. Of course, it did not even smudge, but how was I to explain a freckle? Next he was intrigued with my long red hair. He made clear with signs that he would trade a pony for it. I was sore tempted ~ I have wanted an Indian pony since seeing the Sioux princess. But I was already wearing boy's clothes. What would Mother say if I lost my girl's hair? The brave saw my hesitation and added a beaded necklace and 2 bracelets to the pot. How I wanted to say yes! But I shook my head no and, yanking on my braids, showed that there was no way to give him my hair, even if I was willing. At that, the Indian unsheathed a big hunting knife and motioned how he could cut off the hair. Mother blanched at the sight of that blade. I did not relish the thought of my throat being slit, either, so I showed the Indian what I feared with frantic gestures. He was determined to have my hair, though, and patiently demonstrated how he would cut, with the back of the knife next to my neck and the blade facing away. Mother was so worried he would do anything to get that hair, she hissed at me to trade. So I did. And he was very gentle and careful. He walked away,

The Indians seem to use beads as money.

I saved a tress, to Mother's satisfaction.

Prudence thought I was terrified to have my hair cut. She sought to comfort me by offering to set what hair I have left in curling papers. My hair will never look as nice as hers, but she can try.

I named my pony Spot, since he is spotted as only Indian ponies are. When Will saw him, he was so jealous, he said he wished he were a girl, for he would gladly trade his carrot top for a pony. The trade was worth it just to hear Will pine to be a girl!

well satisfied, but I got the best of the bargain. I can always grow more hair, and for now I have no snarls or tangles to comb out. Best of all, I have my own pony to ride into California!

I gave one bracelet to Frank since I promised him treasure.

August 5, 1850

River crossings are the worst part of this trip. <u>Nothing</u> has been as dangerous or as frightening. Yesterday we forded the Green River. It is not as wide as the Platte but deeper and swifter.

To prepare, the men cut green willow saplings and used them to raise the wagon beds so our provisions would not get flooded. Once the wagons were ready, we drove the yoked teams into the water so they could swim us over. It was terrifying to see the oxen struggling mightily to pull us through the powerful current. Sometimes just the tips of their noses were visible. Vigor and Valor are so weak from months of scant feed and rest, I feared they would drown, pulling us down with them. Mother's mouth was set tight, and I had a knot in my stomach the size of a

14-inch saplings are secured to wagon and wheel beds with bolts and ropes.

The wagon looks like it is on stilts. Even raised this high, the lower layers inside got wet. It took days to dry everything out.

I was so proud of Emma, I gave her my Pawnee necklace. I wonder if I would have been as quick-thinking as her.

Lucky, too, that most of their food was in the other wagon. They did lose some flour, but we all gave them some of our own. I pray we have no more big rivers to cross.

We are all low on provisions, and Pa says once we reach the Humboldt River, there will not be much game to hunt.

muskrat. Even Pa looked pinched with worry. But our team has never let us down. We made it across and waited anxiously for the others.

Watching them was as miserable and wrenching as our own crossing. All landed safely until Mr. James Sunshine started over. Somehow the body of the wagon floated off the wheel bed. The current drove it downstream, but Pa, Mr. Elias, and the other Mr. Sunshines snagged it and pulled it to shore. It had nearly sunk. The water was so high that Emma yelled at Frank and Caroline to hold fast to the wagon bows to keep their heads above water. Baby George she grabbed herself with one arm, holding him above the flood, while she gripped the wagon bow with the other. Emma is no bigger than a bar of soap after a week's wash, but she held that baby tight and no one was hurt.

August 12, 1850

Mother is not feeling well and needs to lie down, so I have been driving the team. We mark our fifth month on the trail, and it has been rough going, zigzagging across the Bear River valley. As if to inspire us despite the difficulty, the mountain scenery is spectacular, meadows bright with flowers, thundering waterfalls. It feels like we are on top of the world, the sky is so close and the air so clear and cold.

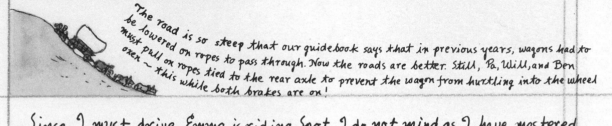
The road is so steep that our guidebook says that in previous years, wagons had to be lowered on ropes to pass through. Now the roads are better. Still, Pa, Will, and Ben must pull on ropes tied to the rear axle to prevent the wagon from hurtling into the wheel oxen ~ this while both brakes are on!

Since I must drive, Emma is riding Spot. I do not mind as I have mastered cracking the whip ~ and without losing any skin, either! Pa is proud, but Mother sees it as another sign she is losing me to rough frontier ways.

August 20, 1850

We crossed another desert, passing many dead cattle on the way. I stopped counting after 50. It was a miserable sight, but our own oxen plodded faithfully through. Six cows and two spare oxen joined the carcasses, but we made it to water with all the teams alive.

Mr. Bridger was so eager to drink, that before watering his stock (that he left to Simon, of course), he rushed to the stream. As he bent over to drink, the famous pistol fell out of his belt, the striking pin hit a rock, and the gun shot a bullet, hitting its owner at the shoulder. The bullet just grazed him, but Mr. Bridger moaned loud enough to wake the dead. (And the curses he rained upon that gun!) Now he claims he is too wounded to do anything but sit in his wagon.

Simon and I have cracker whip (when we stop for food and rest. Simon is more accurate with the whip, but I am better at making a loud crack!)

August 25, 1850

We passed where the Oregon Trail splits, Pa says. The right fork leads to Oregon, the left to California. We took the left, and it has been rocky ever since. The road is not really a road, just large

The wind blows dust everywhere, drying and cracking our lips and coating every inch of skin with a film of dirt — I even feel it gritty on my teeth.

a supper of dirt

One evening the wind was so bad that just as we set out our dishes for supper, a strong gust filled our eyes and mouths with sand — not the meal we intended. When we could see again, the dishes had vanished, blown clear away. It took an hour to find them all. By then we had swallowed so much grit, we had no appetite left.

The trail looks like this.

purple stones with no earth in between. The ride is so bumpy that Mother, still feeling ill, is sitting sidesaddle on Prudence's horse while Prudence takes Spot in exchange. She has no choice but to straddle my pony, yet she still looks a lady. How *does* she do it?

George as stew

One jolt sent Frank tumbling into the butter churn. George ended up in the Dutch oven, and Caroline got hit in the eye by a spade.

August 30, 1850

A flood from melting snow washed out the road before us, leaving a sheer drop of 8~10 feet. There was no other way to go, unless we gave up and went back home, but Pa was not worried. We had already crossed two bad rivers, we could manage this.

Mr. Elias set everyone to work, cutting brush and tree limbs and hauling dirt and gravel. If there were no roads, then we would make one! We filled the ditch as best we could, but it was still steep and uneven. Pa thought that with the surest oxen, we could get through, so we made up a team of the best oxen, led by our own Vigor and Valor. (I *knew* they were the best!) Then we rolled the first wagon by hand to the edge of the drop-off, yoked up the team, and tied ropes to the rear axle. The men pulled back on the ropes while the oxen stepped slowly and carefully. Gradually the wagon reached the level road.

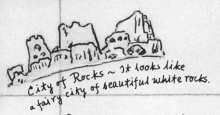
~ wonders of the California Trail ~

"City of Rocks ~ It looks like
a fairy city of beautiful white rocks.

Soda Springs ~ Some are boiling
hot, some cold, some warm, all taste like
ink but are said to have healthy minerals.

Steamboat Springs~
Water gushes ~3 feet high
from solid rock!

One by one each wagon was yoked to the same trusty team and brought down. Not a single wagon tipped over!

The rest of the stock was driven down the narrow path that had not washed out, and we all scrambled down by holding on to vines and bushes (hurrah for my britches!). George and Asa were passed from one person to the next until they were safe on the ground. It was draining work, but by supper we arrived at Thousand Springs Valley and were rewarded with a beautiful grassy place to camp. (And there really are thousands of small springs dotting the valley floor.)

September 7, 1850

We follow the Humboldt River now and can see in the distance the tops of the Sierra Nevada Mountains, white with snow already, to our dismay. Pa says not to fret ~ we are not going to the _tops_ of the mountains, and the pass is still clear. Mother does not say anything, but she is reading her Shakespeare less and her Bible more.

The oxen are thin and tired and our provisions low. We have passed small trading posts, but the prices are too high for us.

My thank-you to Vigor and Valor
for getting all the wagons down ~
I gave them a handful of
precious salt. They
surely earned it!

These trading posts are small shanties with only a few goods for sale ~ sugar, flour, whiskey~ at an outrageous profit.

chewing tough meat ~ more jaw exercise than nourishment

Instead Pa slaughtered a cow, but I had to force myself to eat it as the meat was stringy and sweet. All the stock has eaten lately is sugarcane.

Anyway, we will soon be in California, the land of milk and honey. Only a little farther to go.

September 12, 1850

Ben, Emma, Lee, and Mrs. Della Sunshine are all sick, not from cholera, I think, but from the brackish water we drink. Mother doses everyone, though she is still not well herself. But she said not to fret. This is not sickness. She is with child. And though her belly is big, her face is thinner than ever.

Everyone seems low and worried. Will and I try to cheer up the company by reading from <u>Twelfth Night</u> (no tragedies now!), and Simon fiddles sprightly tunes. Even Prudence does what she can. Last night she popped some corn in the Dutch oven and we had a rare treat.

September 28, 1850

The Humboldt Sink lies before us, an odd, depressing sight. Instead of joining another river

Mother swears by this tonic, but all I can warrant is that it tastes dreadful.

Dr. Biddle's AMAZING BITTERS Elixir of Life

Will borrowed some shawls from the Mrs. Sunshines to make his dress for <u>Twelfth Night</u>. He made a lovely girl in the role of Viola and an even better girl pretending to be a boy when Viola so disguises herself (though he joked that I was already dressed for that part!).

or emptying into a lake or sea, the Humboldt River spreads out in shallow ponds and sinks back into the ground. Beyond it is the great desert, and then the Sierras rise up sharply. If anything feels like the edge of the earth, this does.

Humboldt Sink ~ The water is crusted with alkali, but that is all there is to drink.

We plan on crossing the desert tonight when the cool darkness will make it easier for our oxen to bear. The men are cutting sugarcane to feed the stock on the way and every empty vessel is being filled with water. To ease the weak oxen, we must lighten the load so our cookstove stays here (we can always dig a trench and cook over that), as does the trunk of good china. Mother lovingly bid good~bye to each piece, but Pa promised to come back for it later. Mr. Henry Sunshine wants to leave a heavy chifforobe, but Mrs. Sunshine insists that since it made it this far, it can make it a little farther.

September 30, 1850

We traveled all night through a nightmare landscape. Lee and Daniel led the way with lanterns, but the moon was bright enough to show us the dead cattle, horses, and mules strewn everywhere, along with objects left behind by desperate emigrants.

Adding vinegar or cornmeal to the water helps to purify it, but it does not improve the vile taste.

for what fits in my pockets. I cannot weigh down the oxen with even a button weight.

I worked to take the box, but I only have room

I drew our china here, so even if Pa does not go back for it, Mother will have a keepsake of it.

There were whole wagons, trunks, furniture, bedding, tools, a catalogue of goods. Emma and I went on a treasure hunt, pretending we were exploring sunken pirate ships on the sandy sea bottom. We tried to turn the stench of rotting carcasses into the briny smell of seaweed (as we imagined it), but it was hard not to feel suffocated by the stink of death.

Just before dawn we came to some hot springs, the halfway mark. We stopped to feed and water the stock (with water we brought — the springs were too scalding to drink from). Many of our cattle had added their bones to the desert's riches. Here Mrs. Sunshine's chifforobe joined the other abandoned furniture.

We kept on tramping as the sun rose higher and the day grew hotter. In the scorching light, the desert seemed endless. Dead, bloated cattle lay everywhere, ours among them. There were graves, too — sad to think that people made it so far only to die in the bleakest place of all.

This was the only time during the whole journey I heard Mother cry. She sobbed softly, but I heard her still. I do not know if she wept for those buried in that wasteland or for us. What if the desert were longer than the guidebook said?

buttons from a button box

I stashed this wee book of poetry ~ I am ravenous for books to read. I miss them much more than baths! I also found a man's watch fob and a soft~leather edition of Shakespeare's sonnets. I will give that book to Mother when we reach Sacramento. She will be pleased to see I have brought some civilization with me after all.

Emma picked up a doll like this. Wondering what happened to the girl who once loved it, I could not bear to take it.

What if our oxen died? We had run out of water hours ago, and the only thing that kept us walking was the horror of staying where we were.

Then the faintest smudge appeared on the horizon. At first I thought it was a mirage, like those we saw on the flat, wide prairie, but by noon we could clearly see the trees lining the Carson River. The oxen smelled the water and rushed ahead, bellowing madly.

My sturdy Spot reached the river first, but I was close behind. I filled a cup and brought it to Mother, then ran back and threw myself into the cold clear water. My tongue was so swollen and thick, I could barely swallow, so I lay there and let the water seep into me ~ it tasted wonderful!

Pa fretted that the stock would guzzle too much icy water too fast, but he could not tear the parched animals away. I do not know if it was the water or if he simply wore himself out, but good trusty Valor lay down and died. I know he was only an ox, but he was the best ox. Pa said I was right to cry for him, he was so big hearted and gave us so much.

October 3, 1850

I thought the Rockies were mountains, but they are just hills compared to the Sierras. Huge granite rocks tower over us, and the tops of the peaks are so high, clouds hide them. The trail is steep and rocky, the worst yet. After the desert, to face this is almost more than I can

IN MEMORY OF
VALOR
HE GAVE US HIS ALL.

Sometimes the rocks are so large and slippery, the oxen cannot get a purchase on them, but must be pulled up with ropes.

It seemed sad to leave Valor without a grave or marker, so I made him one. At least he did not die in that wretched desert.

We ate wild onions today, our first vegetable since leaving the Platte. I never reckoned something green could taste so good!

bear, but Pa is cheerful, feeling closer than ever to his new farm, and Mother is determined. She will not look back.

Vigor is now our lead ox with Bo as his new partner, and he looks at me as if he understands his responsibility. I wade beside him as we cross and recross the Carson River. Since the riverbed is a jumble of rocks, I guide the oxen through the rough footing. The noise of wheels clattering over is thunderous, but we have not broken an axle yet.

Ben and the others have all recovered, cured, I think, by the freshwater and spectacular scenery. But Mother is worse. She is always tired and very pale. I read to her when I can. Prudence helps, too. She makes compresses for Mother's head and sings to her. I know I should be grateful, but why does she have to be better at everything?

October 10, 1850

We had almost reached the summit when snow flurries stopped us. The road was too slick for the oxen's hooves, but it is a race now between us and the snow. The men worked quickly to shoe the stock, and we were about to go on when Mother said she was too ill to move. It must be that baby weighing her down. The bachelors, Mr. Bridger, and the Sunshine families said they were sorry, but they could not wait. I cannot blame them. Why stay with us and risk a blizzard?

I drew George's portrait so I do not forget his dear baby face. Who knows how old he will be when next we meet.

Emma's quilt patch

Still, I was sad to part with Emma, Frank, and sweet Baby George. We promised to meet again in Sacramento. I gave Emma the quilt patch I had just finished and she gave me hers. To Frank, whom I promised to bring interesting things, I gave the watch fob I found. And to George, since he would eat any keepsake, I just gave a kiss.

October 11, 1850

Last night was lonely, since there was just the Elias family and us. (I never thought to be so glad to have Prudence near! For once she played cards with me instead of tending to Ben or Mother.) In the morning I discovered that our little company had grown by one — last night Mother had the baby! She is tiny and sweet, with deep blue eyes, black eyebrows, and a bald head. Pa insisted on naming her Sierra Nevada — a big name for a wee babe. It seemed like we should celebrate, so I gave Mother the book of sonnets. I could tell she was very pleased.

Mr. Elias started ahead of us so we could go more slowly and rest if Mother needed it. At least the sky is clear, so no snow for now.

October 12, 1850

Before we reached the summit, we had to descend the Devil's Elbow,

portrait of baby
Sierra Nevada

born October 11, 1850

She is so small, Mother dressed her in an old sock of Pa's ~ a clean one, of course!

Sierra's cradle

Pa took the tools out of his toolbox.

a narrow part of the road with a sheer drop on one side and the mountain "elbowing" into the road on the other. Mr. Elias warned that wagons had pitched off the mountain here. It was perilous for Mother to ride, but although she looked much better, she was too weak to walk. I offered to carry Sierra, but Mother insisted on holding her.

I have never seen Pa so anxious. Now we really needed trusty Valor. I walked behind, fearful I would see the wagon careen off the edge any minute. But Vigor and Bo stepped so carefully ~ they seemed to know of their fragile cargo ~ and at last the wagon, Mother, and baby were on safe ground. Mother's face was pinched tight, but Sierra slept through the entire ordeal!

We topped the next rise and were at the summit! Before us lay the Sacramento Valley, like a vision of the promised land. We all cheered, and Mr. Elias lifted the twins, Judith and Florence, up for a better view. Even Mother had to look out the wagon and introduce Sierra to her birthright. We are in California now. The worst is over. Unless it snows.

October 15, 1850

The wind kicked up today. No snow, but bitterly cold. Now I truly miss my good wool dress. Mother and Sierra wrapped themselves in bedding, making a snug nest. I wished I could cozy up with them and

This side of the Sierras is not so gray and bleak, though it is just as grand. There are trees so tall they seem to hold up the sky, and so wide that with all of us holding hands, we cannot reach around the girth.

imagine us all home safe in a cabin, but I must drive the second wagon.

We were following Mr. Elias into camp when Pa's wagon struck a stump, breaking the rear axle. Pa signaled me to swing around him, and I was careful as could be, but I hit a stone, snapping the coupling pole of the second wagon. We were both stuck. I felt lower than a snake.

Mr. Elias helped us bring food and bedding to the campfire so we could eat and sleep. But what will we do tomorrow? I was too fretful to go to bed. Prudence stayed up with me and taught me a new embroidery stitch. I tried to work on my sampler, but my fingers were too numb and my heart too heavy.

October 16, 1850

Mr. Elias suggested that Pa ride to a trading post he knew of to look for help. Meanwhile, he would hurry ahead and send back a rescue team. Prudence did not want to part with us, nor did Mrs. Elias, but Mr. Elias said they could best aid us by going. Prudence begged to stay ~ I have never seen her speak so forcefully to her father. Seeing she could not sway him, she took off her thick wool dress and gave it to me, shivering in her cotton one. I did not want to accept, but she insisted. This parting was much worse than the one before.

washboard ribs ~ not much meat on these bones!

Of all the cattle we started with, there are fewer than a dozen left and pretty sorry-looking ones at that. If we were desperate we could slaughter one for a meager meal.

I know Mother was thinking of the Donners, but Pa was determined to be cheerful. He kissed us all and rode off on Spot, promising to return soon. Now we really are all alone.

October 17, 1850

Although we rested today, waiting for Pa was harder work than trudging through the desert. We have scant food left, so Will and Ben ventured hunting. They came back empty-handed. I made a thin flour soup for supper. Pa has not yet returned.

October 18, 1850

Will thinks we should load what we can on our backs and pack out of here, leaving the stock behind. Mother insists that Pa will return. Supper was our last bit of jerky. Pa is still away.

October 19, 1850

A snapping twig startled me awake. Wolves, I thought, and rushed to Mother and Sierra, still asleep in the wagon. I grabbed the whip, prepared to stave off danger, but when I looked back out the wagon, there was Pa! I ran to him, bawling like a baby, waking up the world, Pa claimed. But he was grinning and so were Ben, Will, and Mother. Only Sierra could not fathom all the fuss.

Pa said when he came to the trading post, the trader directed him

One fewer cow today. We celebrated Pa's return with a beef stew ~ more water than beef, but after flour soup it was a feast.

Our first sight of the famous California gold, and it goes to the new California baby!

Sierra's nugget is soft and not as shiny as I thought gold would be. Mother says she hopes this does not mean Sierra will catch gold fever ~ the miners are sure bit bad by the gold bug.

to a wagon that had broken down and been left behind. It took Pa a day to find it, pitched into a deep gully. He climbed down, hanging on to tree roots, hoping the parts we needed would be whole. They were! But Pa could not carry them and climb out of the gully, so he followed it until it sloped up and he could walk out. Then he circled back to get Spot. Spot did not balk at carrying the long poles ~ that is his Indian training. Pa and Ben fixed both wagons and tomorrow we head on.

October 20, 1850

No more snow, but we have so little food left that we no longer stop at noon but hurry on (if you can rush exhausted, starving oxen). At least the trail is less rocky, though still steep.

We have passed miners searching for gold so I can tell we are in California. No families yet, just lone men intent on panning. One grizzled fellow was so taken with Sierra ~ it had been so long since he had seen a baby ~ that he gave her a gold nugget! He said babies are more rare than gold.

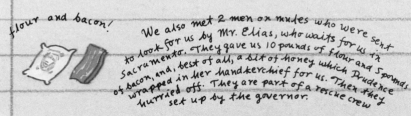

flour and bacon!

We also met 2 men on mules who were sent to look for us by Mr. Elias, who waits for us in Sacramento. They gave us 10 pounds of flour and 5 pounds of bacon and, best of all, a bit of honey which Prudence wrapped in her handkerchief for us. Then they hurried off. They are part of a rescue crew set up by the governor.

The rescue crews search the mountains for late-arriving emigrants. Another train is behind us at the pass. I pray they make it safely. We have been very fortunate.

I cannot recall how it feels to be inside a house anymore.

We passed a schoolhouse ~ oh, dear, we are back in civilization.

October 23, 1850

This morning we woke up early. The guidebook showed that there were only a dozen or so miles ahead, and no one wanted to sleep. We descended the last stretch of 8 miles. The road is smooth and level, dotted with farms and homesteads. We are finally, safely here!

The other families we meet are all so friendly. One fruit seller welcomed us with a watermelon and astonishing news ~ California has just been admitted to the Union. We are not only back in civilization, we are back in the United States of America!

Pa grinned at Mother and handed her the first slice of melon. Tomorrow we would find our homestead. Today, I looked back at the wagon, at our family, bigger by one. We were not at the edge of the world after all. Not in a strange place. Not in between anymore. We finally were somewhere. We were home.

I saved some seeds so we can plant watermelon in our new California garden. But first I will give some to Prudence.

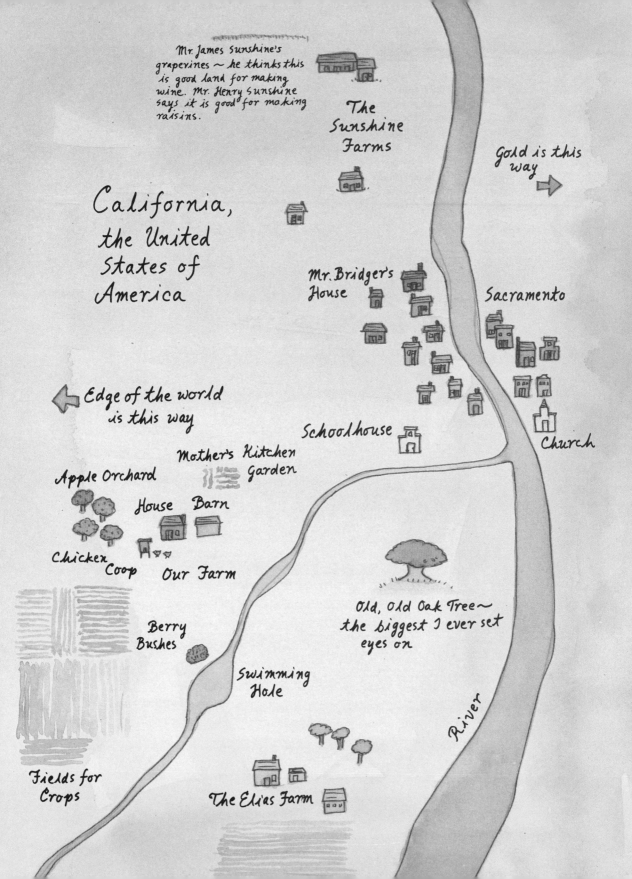

Rachel's Journal is a work of fiction based on the lives of many of the families who traveled the Oregon Trail from 1846 to 1868. While all of the characters in the book have been created by the author's imagination, the book is meant to provide a sense of what it would have been like to live then. It does not and is not meant to represent the experiences of any one person who actually lived.

No part of this publication may be reproduced in whole or in part, or stored in a retrieval system, or transmitted in any form or by any means, electronic, mechanical, photocopying, recording, or otherwise, without written permission of the publisher. For information regarding permission, write to Harcourt Brace & Company, 6277 Sea Harbor Drive, Orlando, FL 32887-6777.

ISBN 0-439-13342-4

Copyright © 1998 by Marissa Moss. All rights reserved.
Published by Scholastic Inc., 555 Broadway, New York, NY 10012,
by arrangement with Harcourt Brace & Company.

SCHOLASTIC and associated logos are trademarks
and/or registered trademarks of Scholastic Inc.

12 11 10 9 8 7 6 5 4 3 2 1   9/9 0 1 2 3 4/0

Printed in the U.S.A.   23

First Scholastic printing, September 1999

The illustrations in this book were done in watercolor, gouache, and ink.
The display type was hand lettered by Tom Seibert.
The text type was hand lettered by Marissa Moss.
Designed by Judythe Sieck and Rachel

Author's Note

Rachel's story is fictional, but it is based on many actual experiences of overland emigrants between 1846 and 1868. Diaries kept by women and children were written from a very different perspective than those of men. Children, especially, viewed the trip along the Oregon Trail as one long adventure, and I tried to capture some of that excitement in this book. Every major incident Rachel describes actually happened to someone traveling along the trail, from the falling dentures to the Platte River crossing.

My research for this book also led me to pioneer guidebooks from the period, in which chapter topics ranged from "Indian Pantomime" to "How to Set Up a Tent." Of the general histories, I especially recommend Emmy Werner's _Pioneer Children on the Journey West._

Many of the journals I read in manuscript form reside at the University of California at Berkeley in the Bancroft Library. They are available to those curious enough to seek them out. From a twelve-year-old girl to an eighteen-year-old woman, the voices I discovered in these diaries were eager, courageous, and adventurous. I hope _Rachel's Journal_ conveys their pioneer spirit.